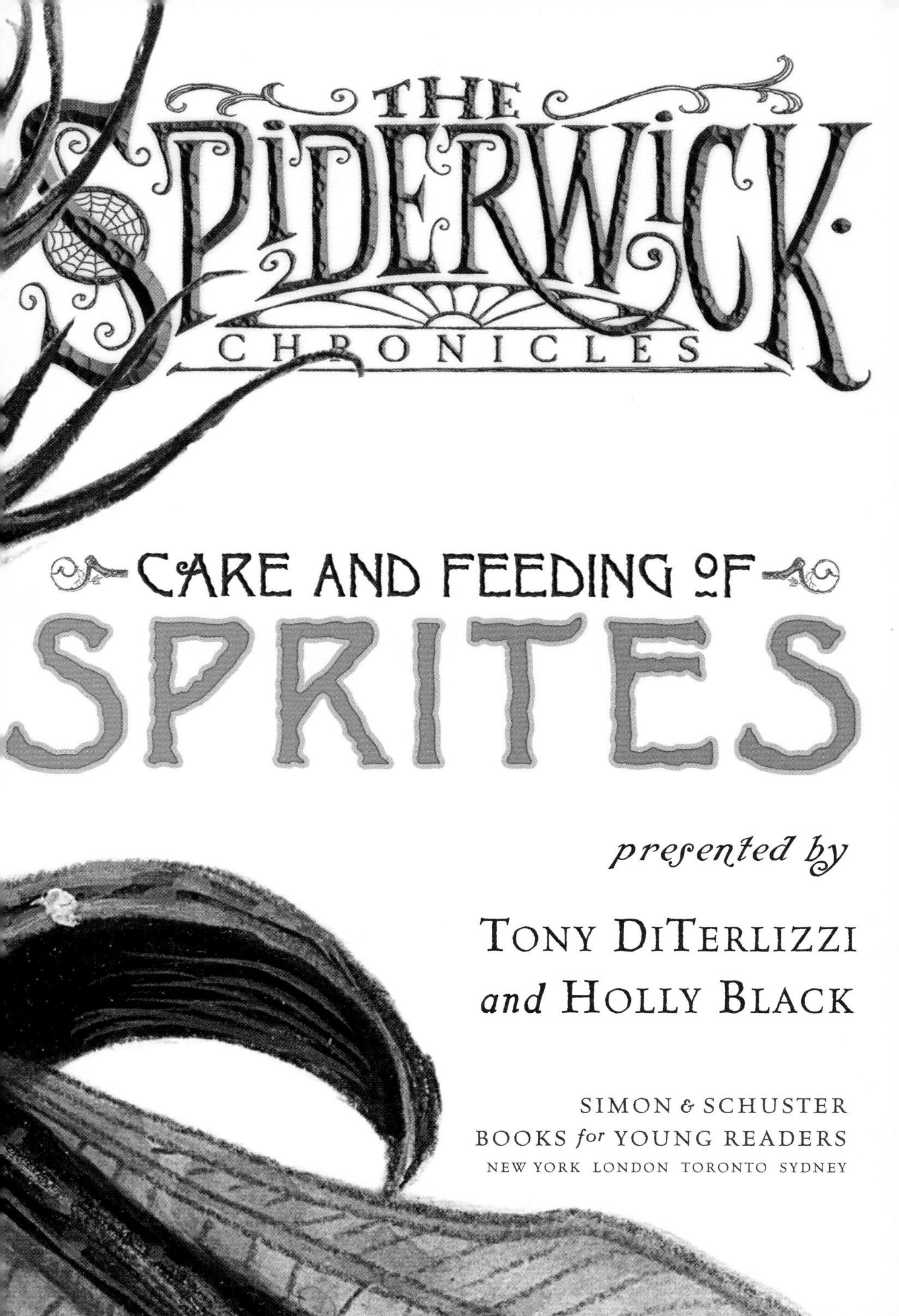

CARE AND FEEDING OF SPRITES

presented by

TONY DITERLIZZI
and HOLLY BLACK

SIMON & SCHUSTER
BOOKS *for* YOUNG READERS
NEW YORK LONDON TORONTO SYDNEY

For Goblin,
Chamberlain,
Fizzgig,
and all our other pets,
past, present, and future
—T. D. & H. B.

SIMON & SCHUSTER BOOKS FOR YOUNG READERS
An imprint of Simon & Schuster Children's Publishing Division
1230 Avenue of the Americas, New York, New York 10020

Book design by Michael Nelson
The text for this book is set in Celestia Antiqua.
The illustrations for this book are rendered in mixed media.
Manufactured in the United States of America
2 4 6 8 10 9 7 5 3
CIP data for this book is available from the Library of Congress.
ISBN-13: 978-1-4169-2757-0
ISBN-10: 1-4169-2757-3

Dear Holly and Tony,

Thank you for the package with all the letters and drawings from fans. They're pretty amazing, even if most of them are for Jared. He's completely obnoxious now, always talking about how he's the famous one. If you ever put him in any other Spiderwick books, make sure he has a big pimple on his chin.

I thought you might be interested in knowing about an organization that Aunt Lucinda and I joined: the International Sprite League. Raising, breeding, and showing sprites is much more exciting than keeping lizards or mice or even exotic birds. I was hoping that you could help us put together a handbook, like they have for other pets, so that sprite keeping will be more widely recognized—maybe someday there will even be an international breed standard!

My local sprite club pitched in and put together some information we thought would be helpful. If you could maybe make it sound better and draw some pictures, it would be the coolest thing ever.

Your friend,
Simon Grace

Dear Readers,

We hope that you enjoy this book as much as we enjoyed making it. Even though, at times, we questioned the wisdom of keeping faeries as pets, we've come to see that the people who love sprites are as unique as the sprites themselves.

Sincerely,

Holly Black

and

Tony DiTerlizzi

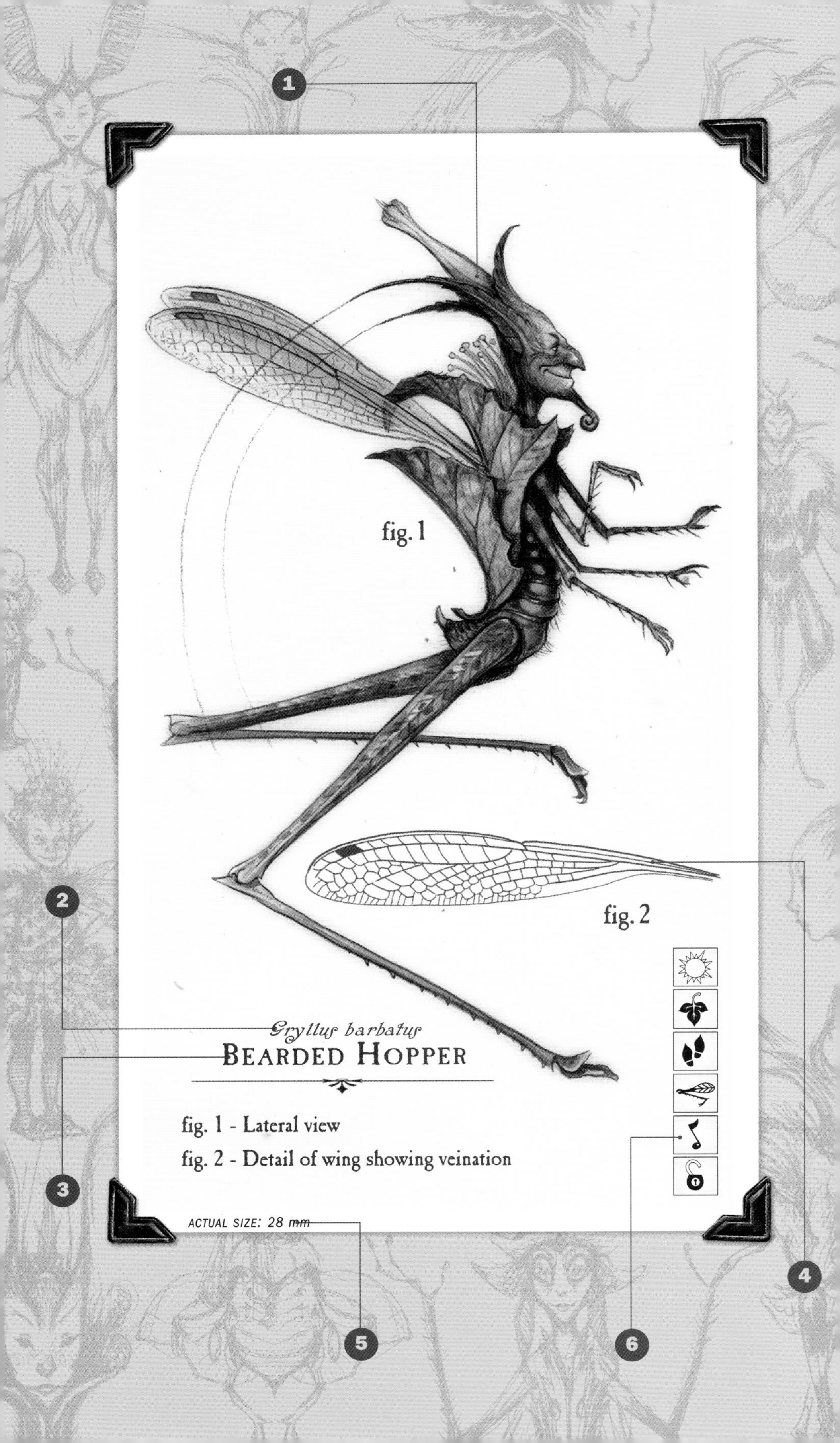

1
fig. 1
fig. 2
2
Gryllus barbatus
BEARDED HOPPER
fig. 1 - Lateral view
fig. 2 - Detail of wing showing veination
3
ACTUAL SIZE: 28 mm
4
5
6

EXPLANATION OF TERMS AND IMAGES USED IN THIS BOOK

1. True appearance of sprite without glamour
2. Scientific (Latin) name
3. Common name
4. Detail of distinguishing physical feature
5. Body height in millimeters

6.

KEY TO SYMBOLS

This key was designed to help you understand the individual characteristics of different sprite species and to help you select the one most suited to your environment.

PREFERRED HABITAT

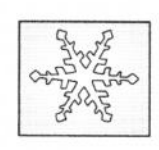 Prefers cold

 Prefers hot

 Prefers wet

 Prefers humid

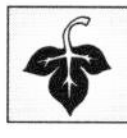 Prefers foliage

PRIMARY LOCOMOTION

 Walks

 Hops

 Flies

GENERAL DISPOSITION

 Cheerful

 Melancholy

 Tricksy

ADDITIONAL TRAITS

 Bites

 Stings

 Sings

 Thinks it can sing

 Clean

 Messy

  Gorges

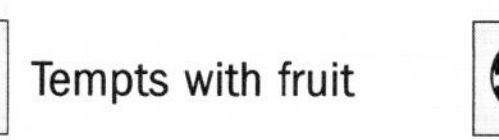 Tempts with fruit

 Causes blooms

Picks locks

Steals infants

Trainable

  Not trainable

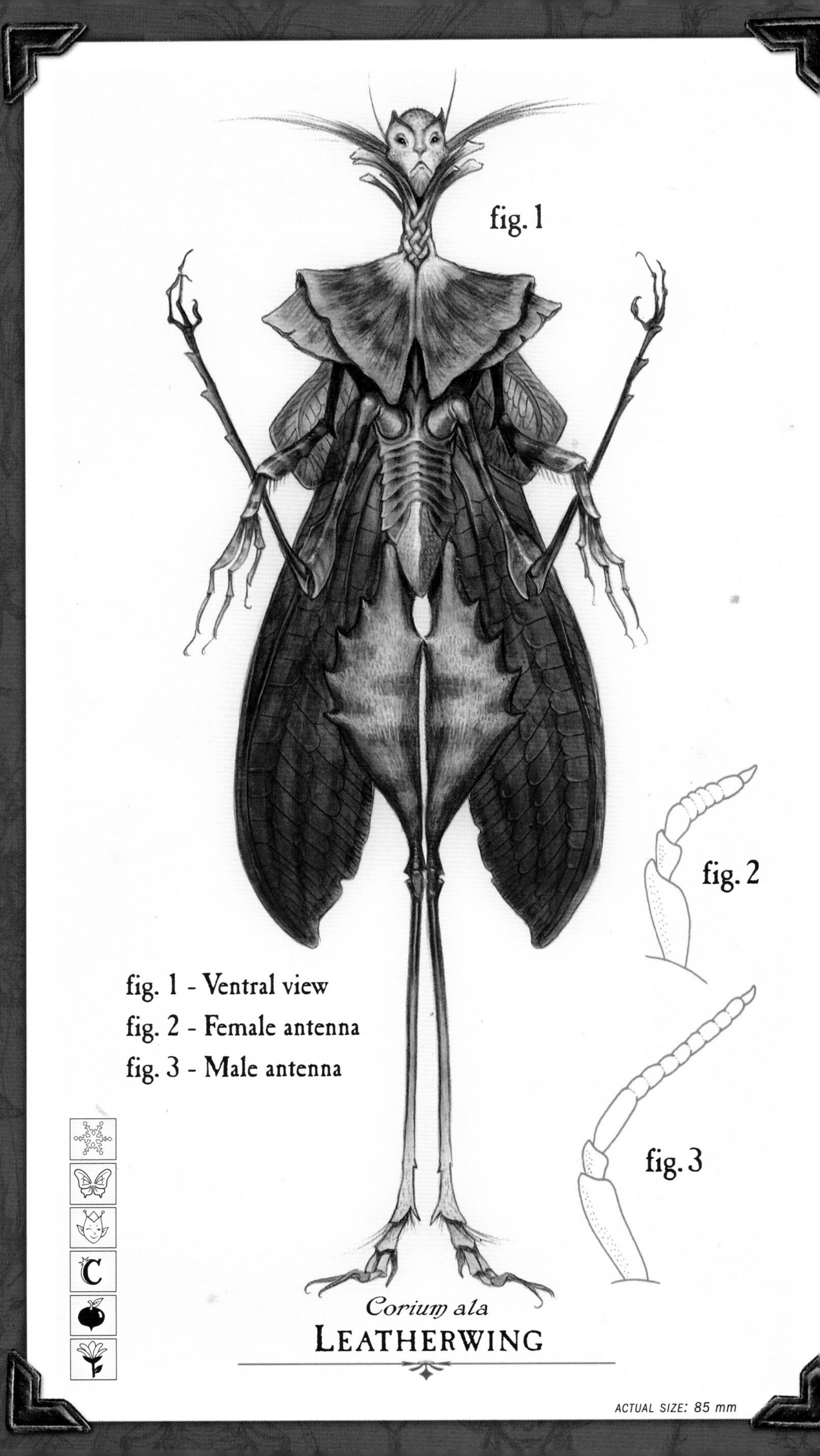
fig. 1
fig. 2
fig. 3
fig. 1 - Ventral view
fig. 2 - Female antenna
fig. 3 - Male antenna
Corium ala
LEATHERWING
ACTUAL SIZE: 85 mm

Section One

THE MAGNIFICENT SPRITE

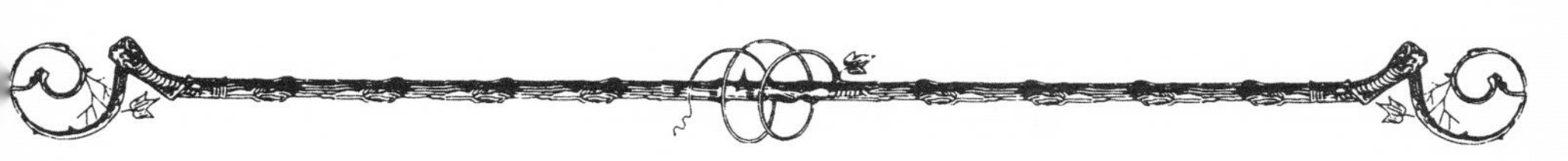

A sprite is a constant reminder of all that is magical. Magnificent creatures with vast variation in color and form, these tiny faeries, some smaller than a toothpick, may make flowers bloom yet can deliver surprisingly fierce bites when threatened.

Their wings are reminiscent of both insects and flowers and their bodies give off a dim glow at night. They have become iconic, even outside the community of sprite fanciers. Their tiny, winged forms are reproduced on jewelry and clothing.

But when thinking about keeping a sprite as a pet, you need to do more than appreciate it. You need to consider the following: How will you acquire your sprite? Where will you house it? How will you be sure it gets the proper exercise and correct nutrition? This book provides simple and easy-to-understand guidelines that, when followed, will help keep your pet both healthy and happy.

DO NOT ATTEMPT TO KEEP A SPRITE IF YOU HAVE NOT ACQUIRED THE SIGHT, THE ABILITY TO SEE FAERIES. ONE MEMBER OF THE SPRITE LEAGUE KEPT A GOBLIN FOR YEARS, NOT KNOWING WHAT HE HAD SIMPLY BECAUSE THE THING REMAINED INVISIBLE TO HIM. ANOTHER HAD AN ENTIRELY EMPTY CAGE THAT SHE SHOWED TO OTHERS WITH GREAT PRIDE, CLAIMING IT CONTAINED A SPRITE BECAUSE THAT'S WHAT THE SPRITE DEALER TOLD HER.

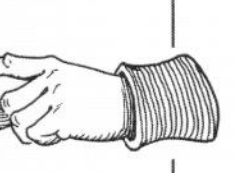

LEFT: Some insect-sprites, like this leatherwing, are not only beautiful in appearance, but extremely intelligent as well. Conversation with them can be quite stimulating.

ANATOMY OF A SPRITE

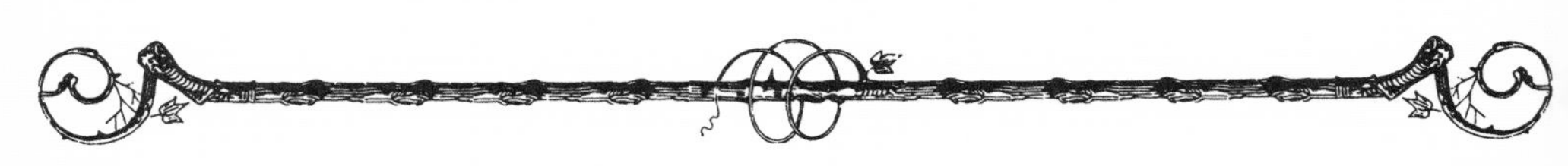

In order to better understand the sprite and to eventually compile lasting breed standards, the International Sprite League uses a common language for identifying the parts of these fascinating creatures.

1. ***abdomen*** – The third of the body divisions, stretching from just below the forelegs to the end of the body and containing the hind legs.

2. ***antennae*** – Feeler-like appendages located above the eyes and tympanum. Some sprites are able to move these individually, and a few have antennae that are jointed enough that they can even use them to gesture. Usually rudely.

3. ***compound eyes*** – Sprites' eyes are composed of many facets. Sprites see in a manner that could be compared to looking at a wall of televisions, with several tuned to different channels.

4. ***forelegs*** – The armlike parts of a sprite, extending from the thorax. Used to pick up items, steal, and slap.

5. ***forewings (petals)*** – When shaped more like a flower or leaf, the wing that starts first on the thorax is called a petal. When not shaped like a flower or leaf, it is called a forewing. Forewings are the mechanism by which sprites can fly. The forewings are aided by the hind wings, if present.

6. ***head*** – The first of the body divisions, the head contains the compound eyes, tympana, and antennae.

7. ***hind legs*** – The leglike parts of a sprite, extending from the abdomen. Used to kick, skip, and walk.

8. ***hind wings (sepals)*** – When shaped more like a flower or leaf, the wing that starts second on the sprite's thorax is called a sepal, after the small leaves under a flower. When not shaped like a flower or leaf, it is called a hind wing. In both cases its primary function is for flight, though males sometimes use it for display. Some sprites do not have hind wings.

9. ***thorax*** – The second of the body divisions, the thorax contains the forewings, the hind wings, and the forelegs.

10. ***tympana*** – Membranes connected to the nervous system, resulting in superattuned hearing. It is best not to gossip about your sprites. Even when you think you are at a sufficient distance, you are probably mistaken.

Basic Sprite Body

fig. 1
fig. 1 - Antenna variations
fig. 2 - Ventral view
fig. 2
Orchis communis
COMMON ORCHID SPRITE
ACTUAL SIZE: 45 mm

SELECTING YOUR SPRITE

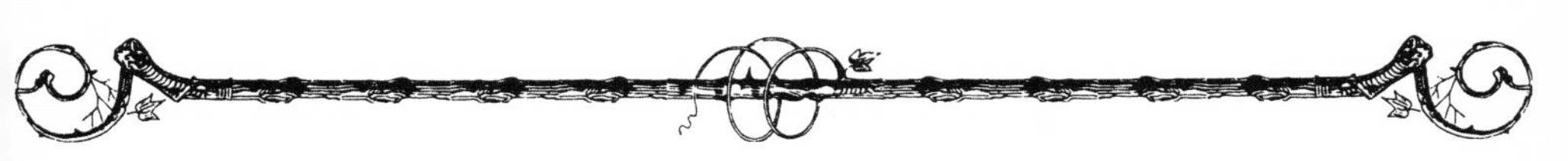

Not only should you look for a sprite that is healthy, but you should select your sprite for the qualities of its breed that are right for you. Many sprite fanciers report feeling an instant bond with their sprite, but for others that bond grows over time. Either way, what is most important is that your new pet fit in with your lifestyle. Consider how many hours a day you have to devote to the care of your sprite and how careful you are willing to be in terms of maintaining the temperature, housing, and diet of one of the more demanding species. You should also consider the preferences of other members of your family if they're going to be helping out with your sprite.

YOUR SPRITE SHOULD HAVE:

- ✓ *BRIGHT, CLEAR EYES*
- ✓ *UNBROKEN WINGS*
- ✓ *AN EVEN NUMBER OF APPENDAGES*

A HEALTHY SPRITE WILL:

- ✓ *FLY AND OTHERWISE MOVE AROUND ITS CAGE*
- ✓ *EAT AND DRINK PROFFERED FOODSTUFFS*
- ✓ *TRY TO ESCAPE*

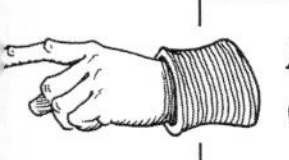

LEFT: Orchid sprites are very delicate and rarely found in the wild. Only the most experienced fancier should attempt to keep them.

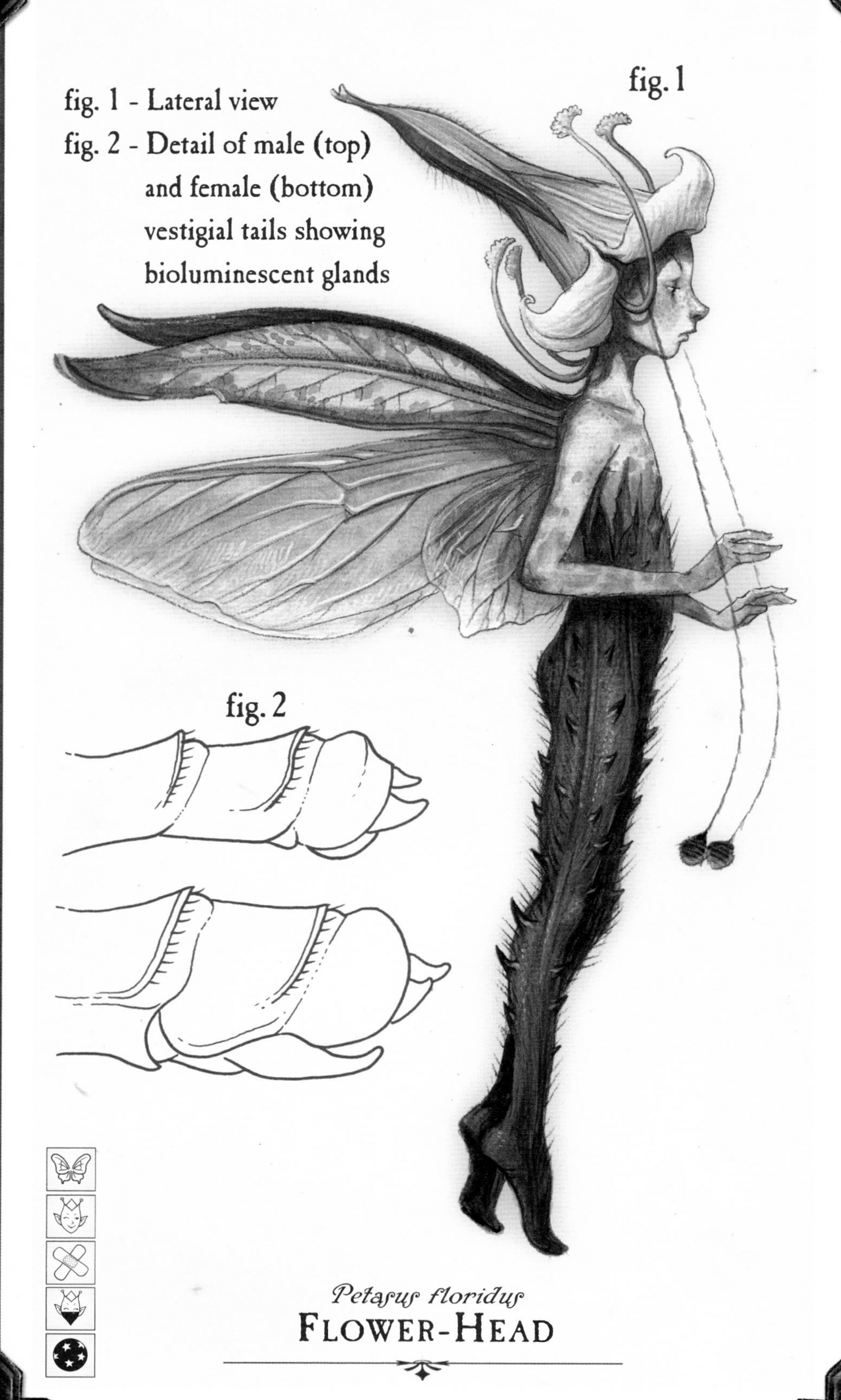
fig. 1 - Lateral view
fig. 2 - Detail of male (top) and female (bottom) vestigial tails showing bioluminescent glands
fig. 1
fig. 2
Petasus floridus
FLOWER-HEAD
ACTUAL SIZE: 45 mm

OBTAINING YOUR SPRITE

There are two ways to obtain a sprite. You can either purchase one from a reputable dealer or catch one on your own. If you prefer to go through a dealer, your local chapter of the International Sprite League may be able to connect you with someone local.

Due to the scarcity of dealers, the skyrocketing cost of sprites, and the dangers of fraudulent sprite trafficking, many people opt to capture their own sprite.

BE CAUTIOUS OF UNSCRUPULOUS SPRITE DEALERS CLAIMING THAT THEY ARE BREEDERS WHO CAN GET YOU HEAVILY DISCOUNTED SPRITES. SPRITES RARELY REPRODUCE IN CAPTIVITY. ALMOST ALL OF THEM ORIGINATE IN THE WILD. GIVEN THAT, THERE ARE FEW LEGITIMATE WAYS TO MINIMIZE COSTS IN ACQUIRING THEM.

NEVER PURCHASE SPRITES THROUGH THE MAIL OR VIA ONLINE AUCTION SITES. MORE OFTEN THAN NOT, THESE SO-CALLED SPRITES ARE FAKES THAT GIVE A BAD NAME TO SPRITE FANCIERS EVERYWHERE. EVEN IF YOU ACTUALLY RECEIVE A REAL SPRITE, IT IS LIKELY TO BE DAMAGED OR TO HAVE SUCH ANNOYING HABITS THAT IT COULDN'T COMMAND FULL PRICE.

AFTER PURCHASING A SPRITE THROUGH DUBIOUS CHANNELS, A MEMBER OF THE SPRITE LEAGUE WAS DELIVERED A LAWN GNOME WITH WINGS TAPED TO ITS BACK.

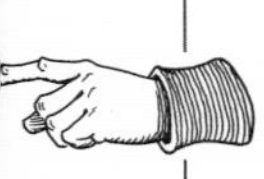

LEFT: Hominid, or humanlike, sprites are generally the most aggressive and clever of all the sprite species. Consequently, they must be regarded with caution.

WHAT'S NOT A SPRITE

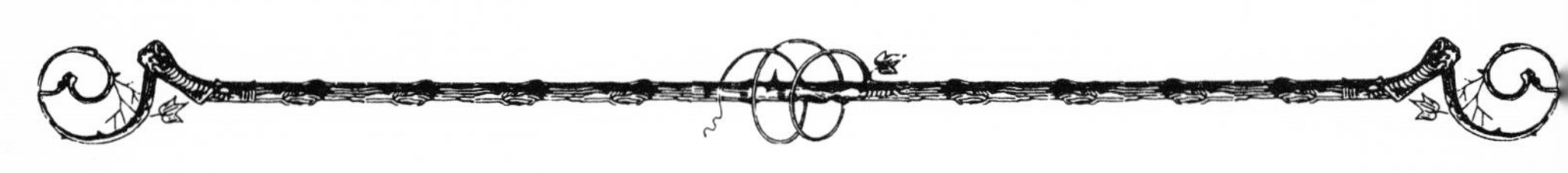

It is easy to be deceived into thinking you've acquired a sprite when what you really have is another kind of faerie. If you discover that you possess any of these creatures, you should release them immediately.

CREATURES OFTEN MISTAKEN FOR SPRITES

GOBLINS – Some varieties of goblins have spritelike growths in the manner of anglerfish. They use the growths as lures, making the rest of their bodies invisible so that only the decoy sprite is showing. One decoy sprite was "caught" and the goblin stayed hidden until dark, when it opened its cage and marauded its owner's house, eating anything that fit into its mouth.

PIXIES – Although pixies and sprites have many similarities, pixies are larger and do not exhibit the magnificent variety of coloration that is seen in the sprite. Also they are even more outrageous pranksters and they tend to gossip more.

WILL-O'-THE-WISPS – If caught and caged, the will-o'-the-wisp will flutter about lazily, and the lawn outside the residence where it is confined will become waterlogged, like the swamp that is the will-o'-the-wisp's natural habitat. Those inside the house when the will-o'-the-wisp is present will become disoriented and will be unable to leave; some will even get lost in corridors and large rooms. Those not in the house will be less and less capable of finding their way home.

RIGHT: The will-o'-the-wisp is a wondrous and dangerous creature. Despite its beauty, under no circumstances should keeping one be attempted.

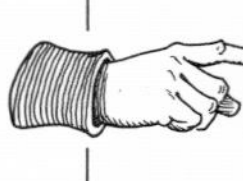

fig. 1

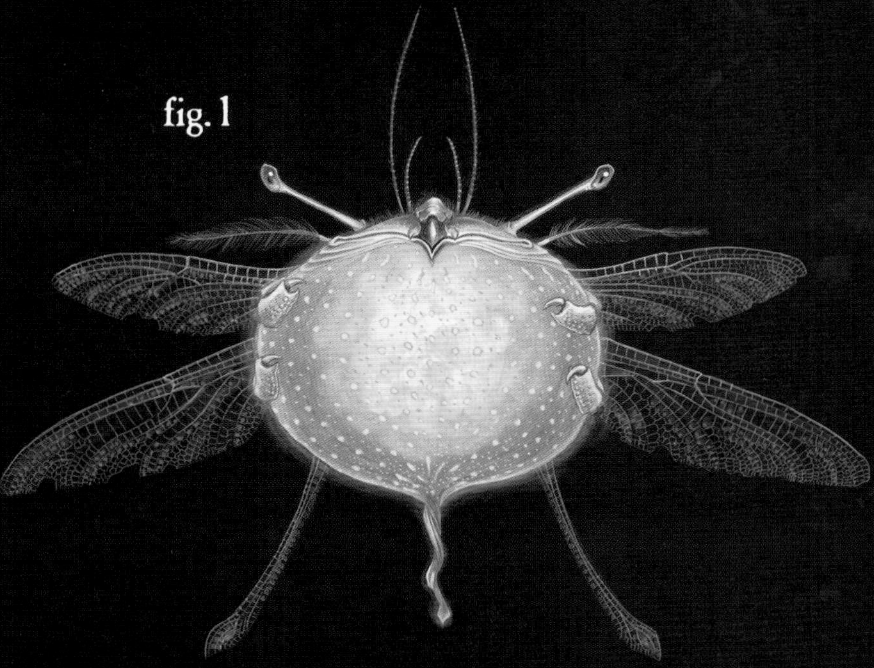

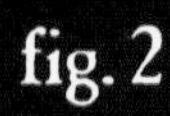

fig. 2

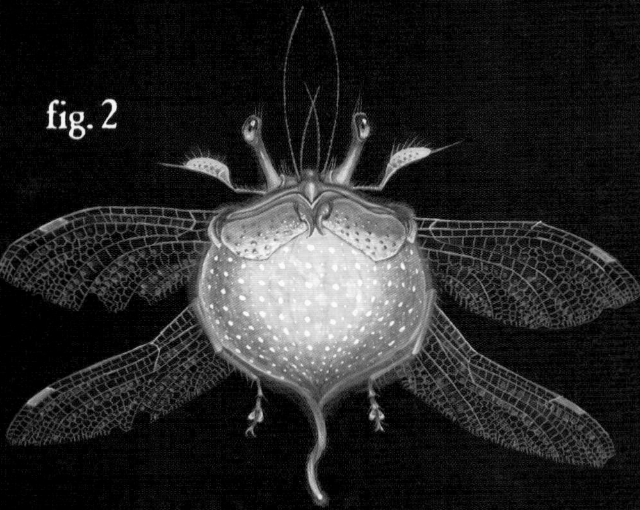

Candentisphaera floccata

WILL-O'-THE-WISPS

fig. 1 - Female

fig. 2 - Male

ACTUAL WINGSPAN: 170 mm (top), 125 mm (bottom)

SEXING YOUR SPRITE

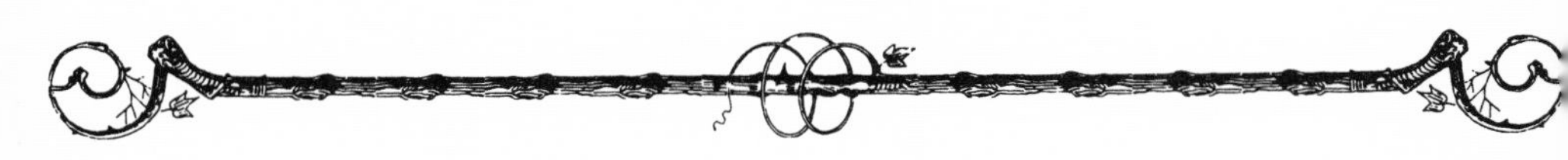

You may want to know if you have a girl sprite or a boy sprite. This is very difficult to determine visually. Your best means is asking.

Politely.

RIGHT: Like crickets and katydids, hopper sprites sing as their primary method of communication. Both males and females are capable of this, each with a different tone and song structure.

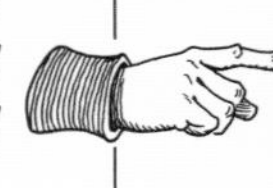

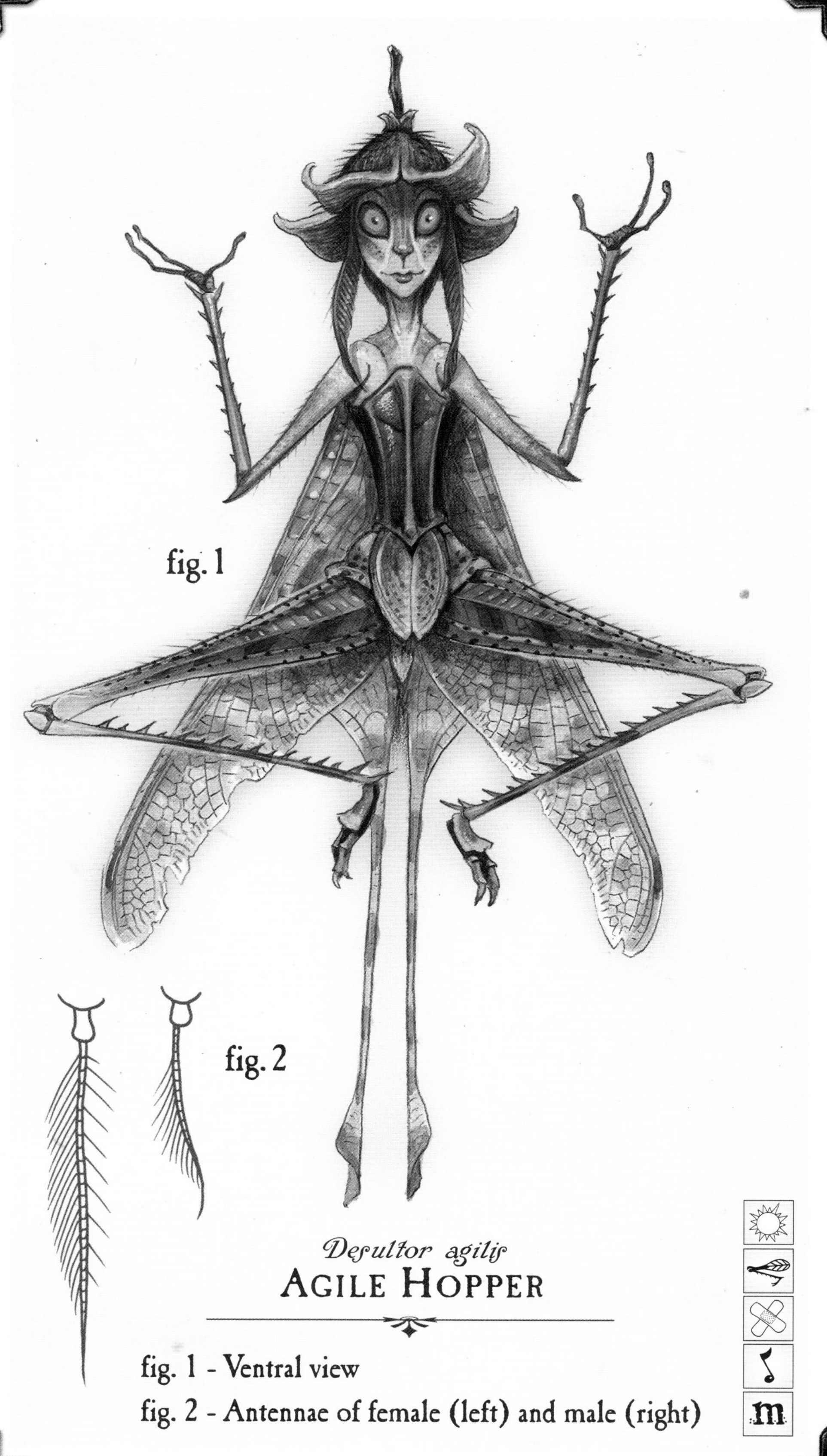

Desultor agilis

Agile Hopper

fig. 1 - Ventral view

fig. 2 - Antennae of female (left) and male (right)

ACTUAL SIZE: 32 mm

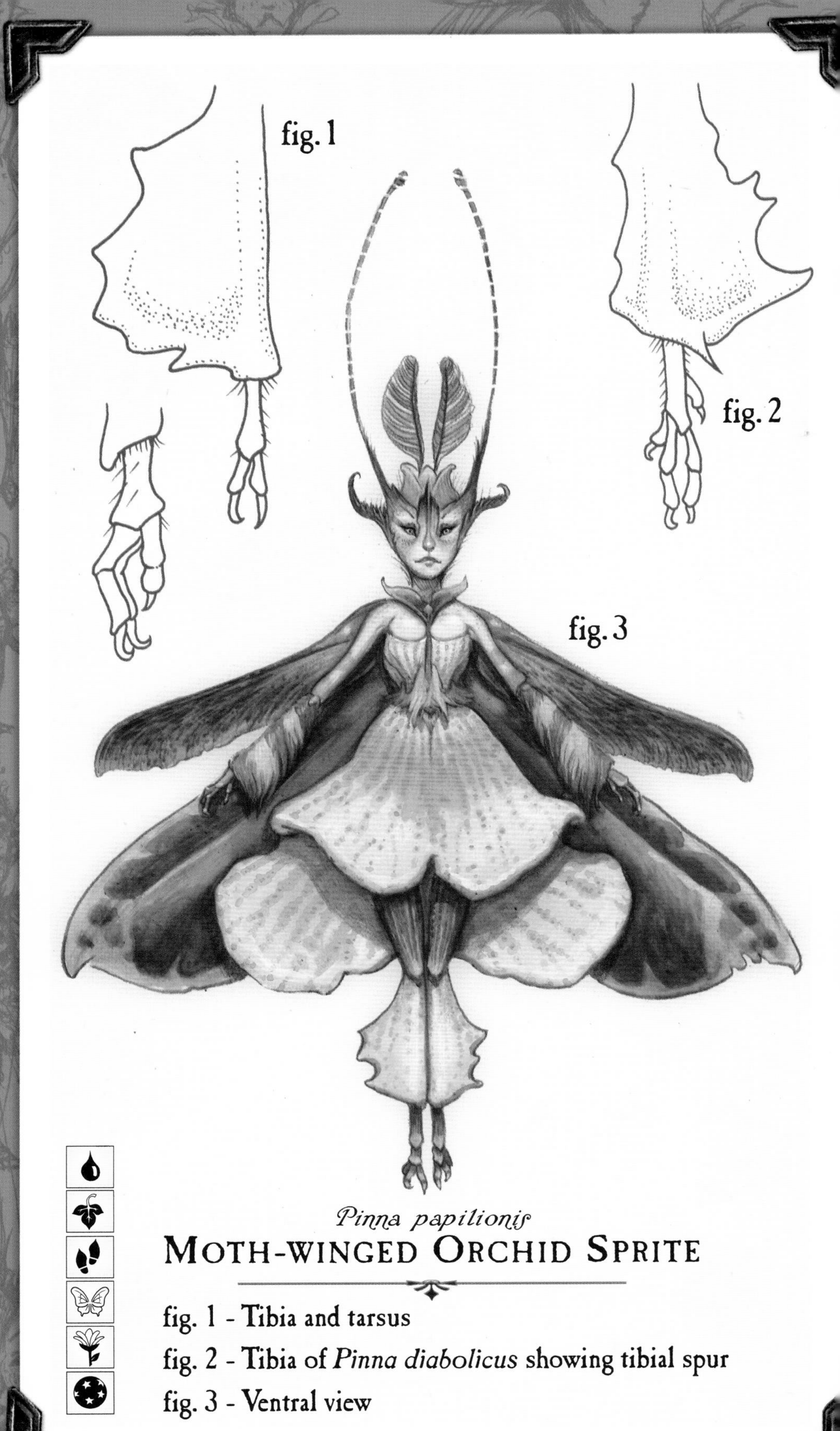

Pinna papilionis

MOTH-WINGED ORCHID SPRITE

fig. 1 - Tibia and tarsus

fig. 2 - Tibia of *Pinna diabolicus* showing tibial spur

fig. 3 - Ventral view

ACTUAL SIZE: 42 mm

HOUSING YOUR SPRITE

It is important to find a cage for your sprite that is both comfortable and secure. There are many different-size cages commonly sold for birds that you can reconfigure to house your sprite with minimum effort. Just make sure they are not made from iron. The most easily available cage is one that has a floor of 18-by-18 inches. This is the minimum size you should consider for your sprite, as it is barely enough room for most varieties to exercise their wings in.

A better size might be an aviary of 30-by-30 inches. This size cage is large enough for branches, a small house, and all the accessories described in section 9. If you are interested in keeping more than one sprite, this is an ideal setup.

IF YOUR SPRITE GOES MISSING, THE FIRST THING YOU SHOULD DO IS SECURELY CLOSE ALL WINDOWS AND DOORS. AFTER THIS, LOOK FOR HIDING PLACES THAT ARE UP HIGH AND DIM, BUT NOT DARK. YOUR SPRITE KNOWS THAT IT GLOWS SLIGHTLY IN DARKNESS AND WILL TRY TO STAY CLOSE TO LIGHT FOR THIS REASON. LOOK ESPECIALLY CAREFULLY INSIDE GLASS VASES OR BEHIND SCULPTURES.

ONE SPRITE HID FOR THREE WEEKS ON THE LEDGE OF A PARTICULARLY HIGH AND DETAILED STRIP OF MOLDING, OCCASIONALLY SWOOPING DOWN AND FRIGHTENING PASSERSBY.

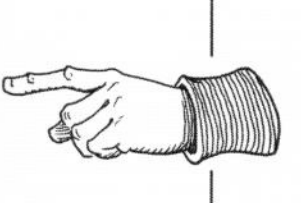

LEFT: Since orchid sprites live in hot and humid areas in the wild, the home you build for one will need to be warm and wet. Also necessary is foliage for cover.

A glass tank is better for tropical species but hard to find in the right height. Another cage type that might be of interest is a ferret cage, which has many levels. Although your sprite will not need the ramps, it may appreciate the size as well as flat planes on which it can cultivate plants or arrange its furniture.

Do not, under any circumstances, house your sprite solely in a dollhouse. Although a dollhouse might seem like a charming location for your new friend, the sprite will be unable to exercise its wings when inside it. Moreover, due to the small size and the flimsy wood usually employed in the construction of these structures, your sprite likely will be able to make an easy escape.

Some keepers feel they have built enough trust between themselves and their sprite to allow the sprite to perch outside its cage for limited periods of time. Most, however, find this inadvisable, as sprites are likely to use this time to execute pranks that will only be discovered much later.

RIGHT: Dragonfly-like sprites are almost constantly on the wing. You'll need a large domicile with plenty of flying area to keep them happy.

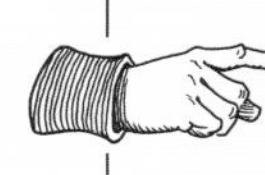

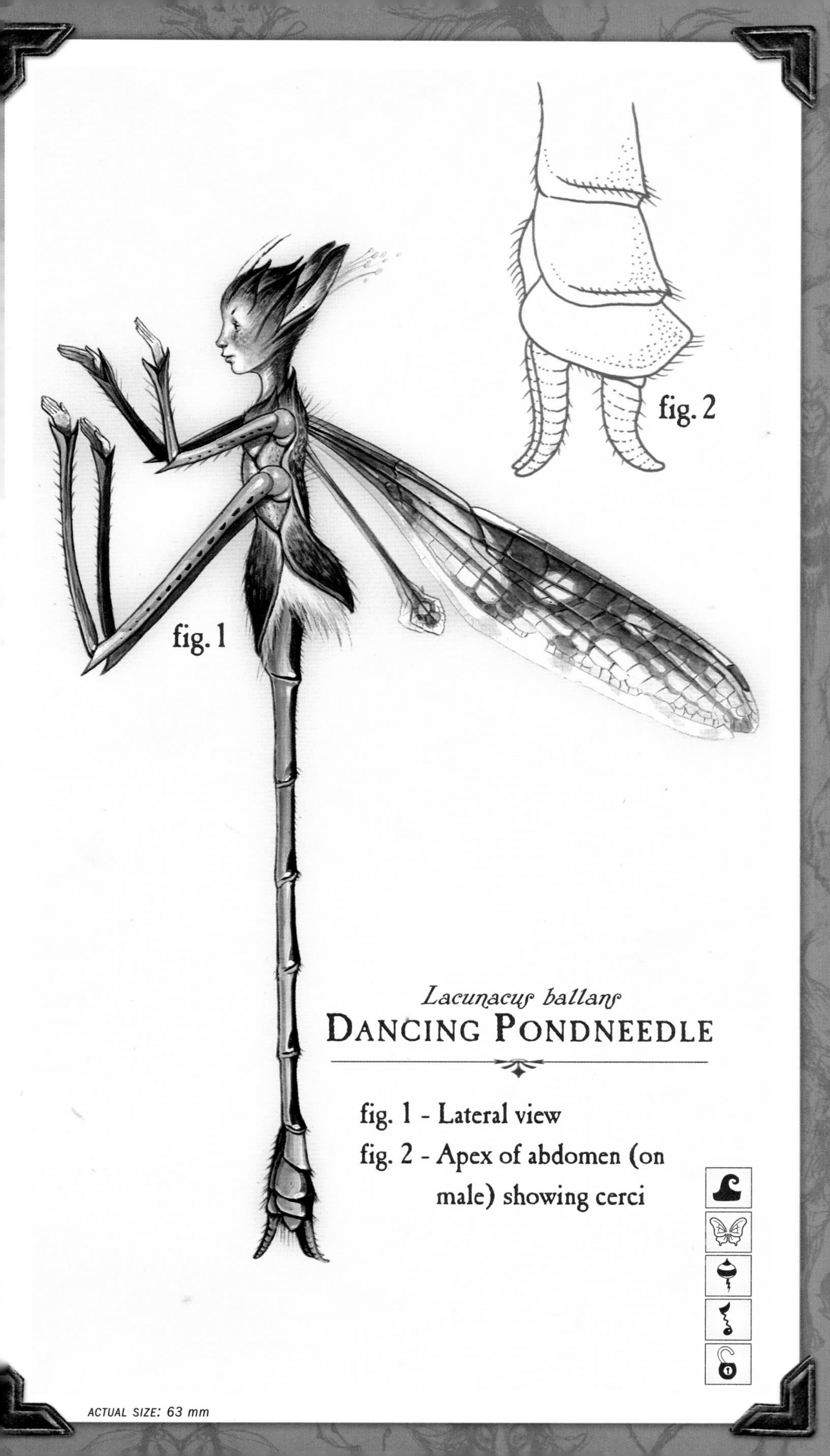
fig. 2
fig. 1
Lacunacus ballans
DANCING PONDNEEDLE
fig. 1 - Lateral view
fig. 2 - Apex of abdomen (on male) showing cerci
ACTUAL SIZE: 63 mm

Section Eight

PROPER NUTRITION FOR YOUR GROWING SPRITE

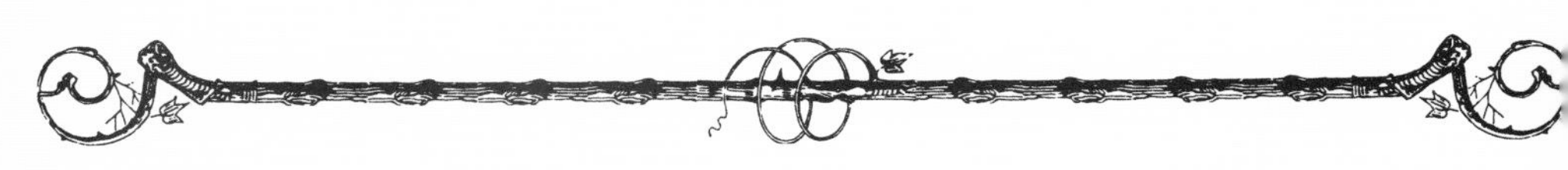

Sprites like to eat clover, the occasional acorn, and the fresh petals of unsprayed flowers. They enjoy drinking pure spring water and, occasionally, a solution of sugar water very similar to simple syrup.

Sprites will sometimes eat human food when it is offered, although it's not the healthiest diet for them. Some sprite keepers give their sprite charges scraps from the family dinner, and sprites have been known to greatly enjoy pies of all kinds, most vegetables, and, occasionally, even cooked meat. What effect this food has on their digestion is unknown.

You should feed your sprite twice daily and always provide plenty of fresh water for its consumption. This water should be different from that available to it for bathing (see section 10).

> *BE CAREFUL NOT TO OVERFEED YOUR SPRITE. MANY SPRITES HOARD EXCESS FOOD, WHICH CAN THEN BECOME MOLDY AND MAKE THEM SICK. OTHER SPRITES SIMPLY WON'T STOP EATING, EVEN IF THEY GET SO LARGE THEY CAN NO LONGER FLY. ONE REPORT SUGGESTED THAT ONE SPRITE EXPLODED AFTER BEING LEFT ALONE WITH A MONTH'S SUPPLY OF FOOD.*

RIGHT: *Blueberry and other fruit sprites have the peculiar habit of carrying around their food on their head. They will eat their berry from the center outward, replacing it with a fresh fruit when they have finished consuming it.*

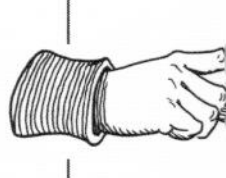

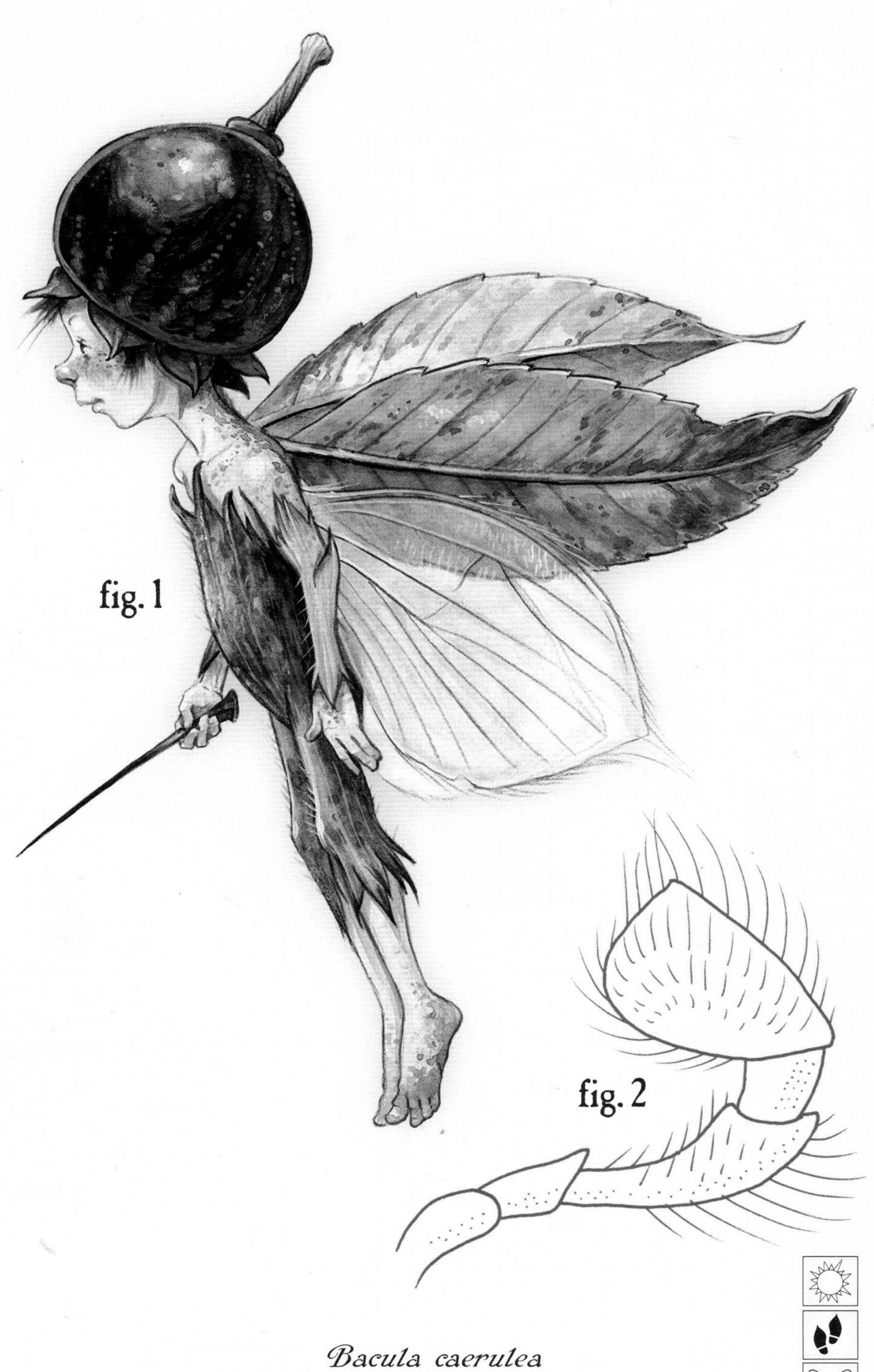

Bacula caerulea

LITTLE BLUEBERRY SPRITE

fig. 1 - Lateral view
fig. 2 - Antenna detail

ACTUAL SIZE: 32 mm

Ala rackhamensis

RACKHAM'S SPRITE

fig. 1 - Lateral view

fig. 2 - *Sphenophorus sp.* weevil

ACTUAL SIZE: 65 mm

SPRITE ACCESSORIES

Aside from their basic necessities, your sprite may desire additional items to enrich its environment.

FOOD AND WATER DISHES – Although it can operate a water bottle like those commonly used by rodents, your sprite will appreciate tableware. Many dollhouse stores sell tiny plates and goblets to the scale of your new pet. Be careful to select those that are not made of iron or steel and are not for display only. If you are a craftsperson, you may prefer to construct your own tableware—perhaps out of acorns or other items familiar to your sprite.

BED – A sprite can sleep comfortably on anything from an abandoned bird's nest to a dollhouse bed. Sprites particularly like to have enclosed beds. These they can reconfigure for themselves to create some privacy. Although you may be disappointed if you can't always watch your sprite in its cage, your impatience is a small price to pay for a happier pet.

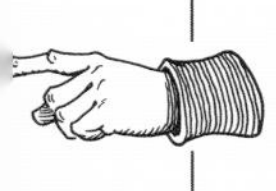

LEFT: Some sprites, like Rackham's sprite, enjoy accessorizing with petal ruffs and pets of their own. The more you spoil your sprite, however, the more high maintenance it is likely to become.

PLANTS – Like many pets, sprites greatly benefit from plants growing at the base of their cage. They will tend these plants on their own, only requiring occasional assistance from you. Moreover, they will be able to use these plants to make clothing, tableware, and even bedding if needed.

CLOTHING – Sprites enjoy making their own clothing from flowers, leaves, and bark. You can provide these raw materials with the expectation that your sprite will fashion its own garments, or you can commission cunning outfits and hope your sprite will be receptive. Many a young girl delights in dressing up her sprites in the manner of popular fashion dolls. Readers of this book should be reminded that sprites are wild beings and unlikely to react well to such treatment.

ENTERTAINMENT – Providing rich sources of amusement for your sprite will keep it from becoming bored and lethargic. Sprites are very fond of music, and a radio nearby will keep them amused for hours. You might also consider giving them paperback books. There are stories of sprites who can operate cell phones and tiny pocket computers, but this seems unlikely as sprites are not fond of technology.

OTHER – Your sprite will also appreciate branches to climb on, a bathing area, and perches on which to land. It may also desire to keep pets of its own, such as beetles, mice, or even small birds. But be sure that your sprite is a responsible caretaker; otherwise you could wind up with two pets.

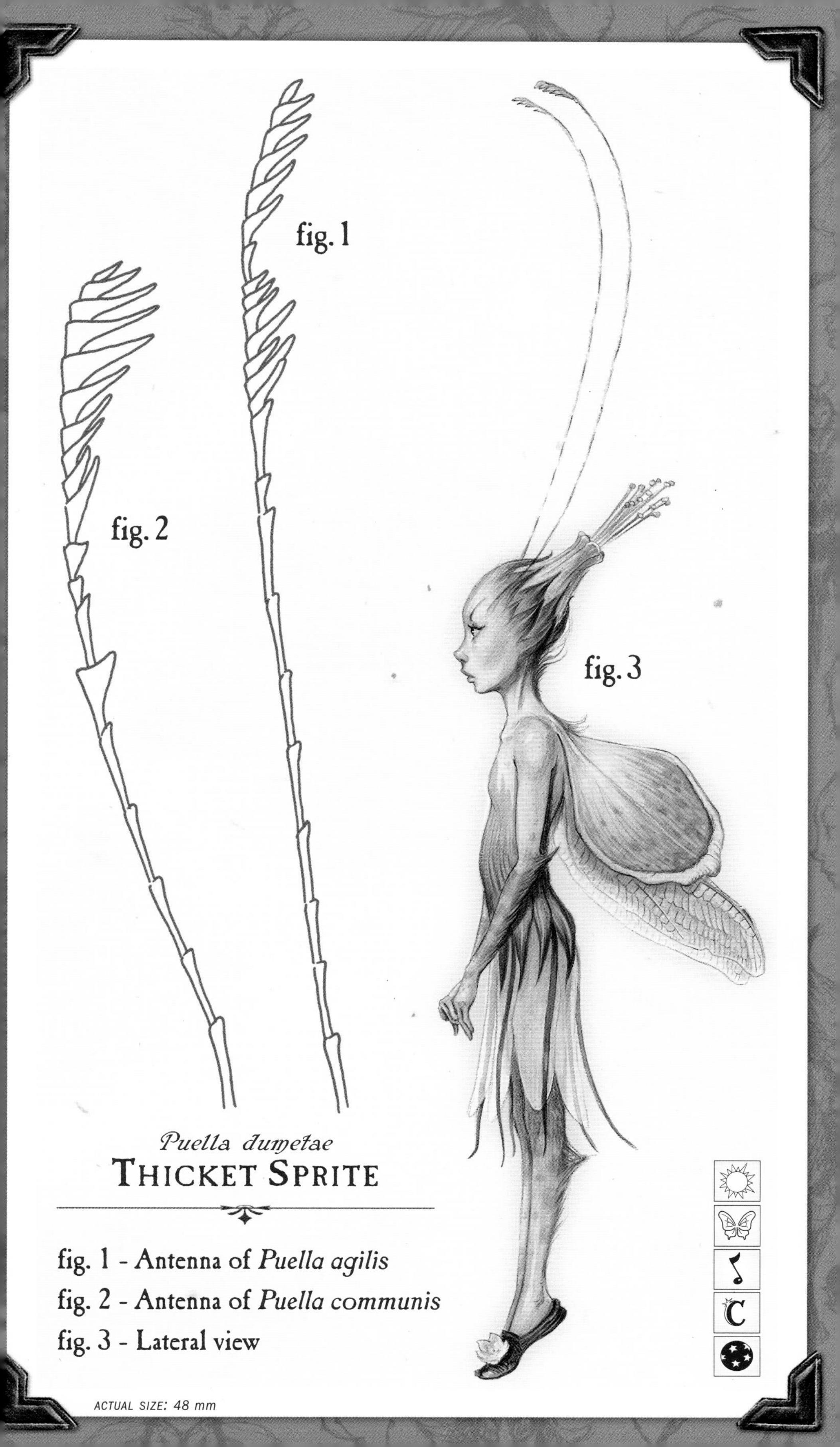

Puella dumetae

THICKET SPRITE

fig. 1 - Antenna of *Puella agilis*
fig. 2 - Antenna of *Puella communis*
fig. 3 - Lateral view

ACTUAL SIZE: 48 mm

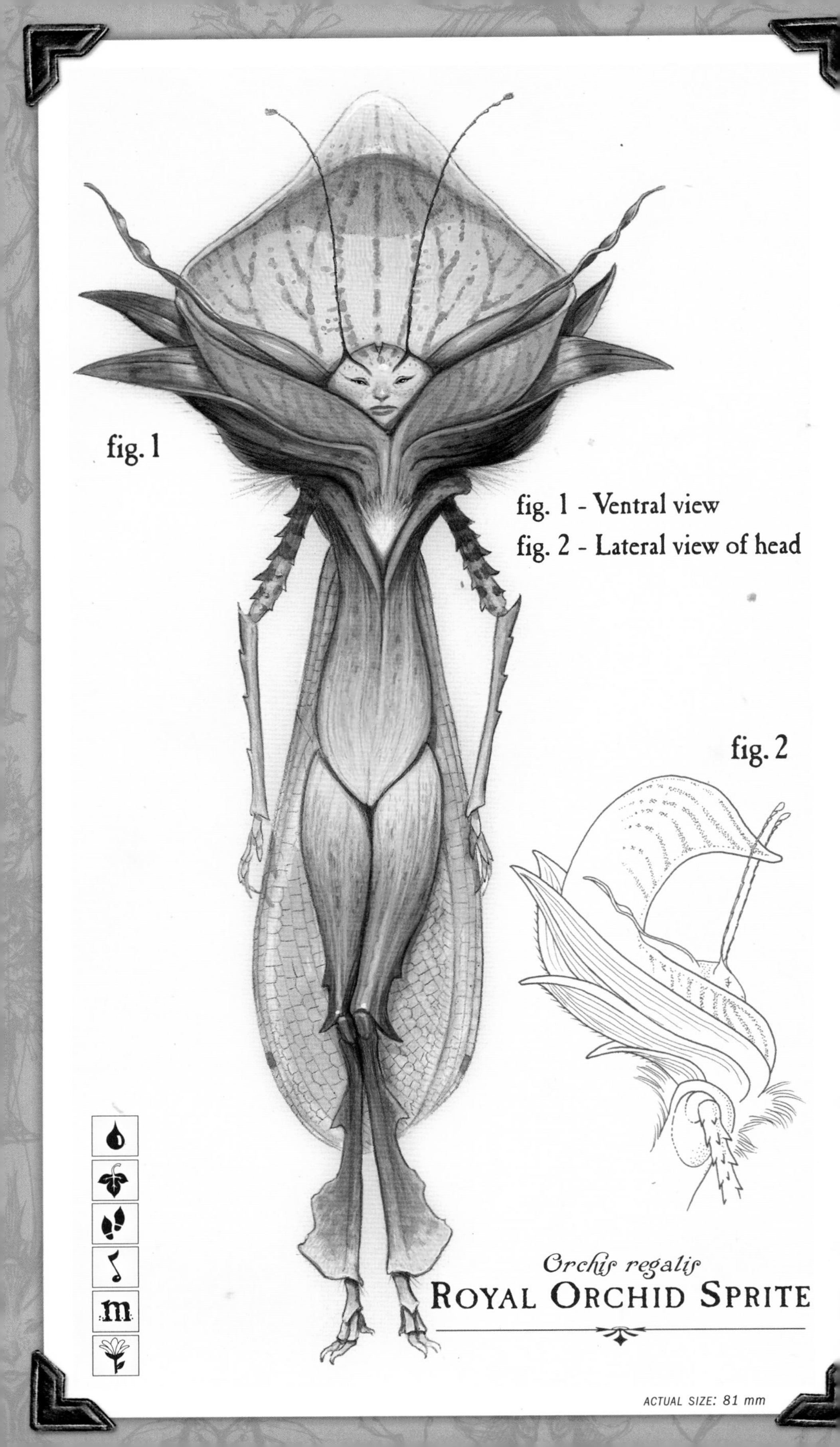
fig. 1
fig. 1 - Ventral view
fig. 2 - Lateral view of head
fig. 2
Orchis regalis
ROYAL ORCHID SPRITE
ACTUAL SIZE: 81 mm

GROOMING YOUR SPRITE

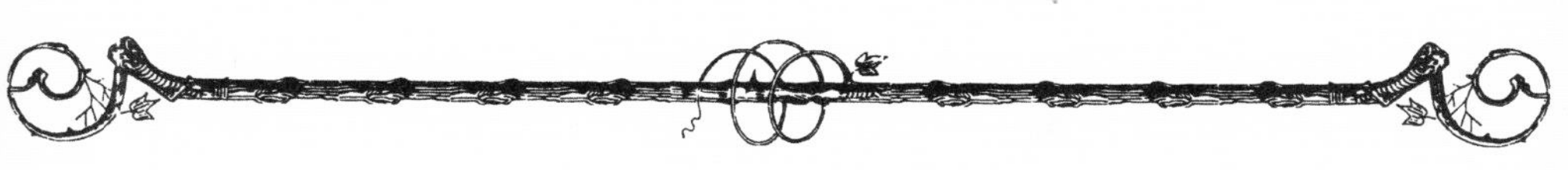

In general, sprites are self-sufficient, but some are more inclined toward grooming themselves than others. Providing your sprite with tiny combs and water in which to bathe might be enough. But if you have a particularly filthy sprite who will not bathe, misting him or her with water will most likely have the desired effect. A few sprites secrete a kind of sticky sap and require regular immersion baths before handling.

Many sprite owners find bath time to be a good opportunity for bonding with their pet and for encouraging it to feel comfortable with being handled. You can also use such time to check your sprite for any cuts or scrapes or torn wings. Do not attempt to perfume or use scented soap on your charge, as sprites are severely allergic to most chemicals.

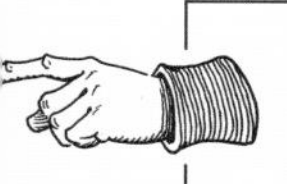

LEFT: Some exotic sprites have special grooming needs, especially if they have hard-to-reach folds. They may need you to gently clean them with a cotton swab.

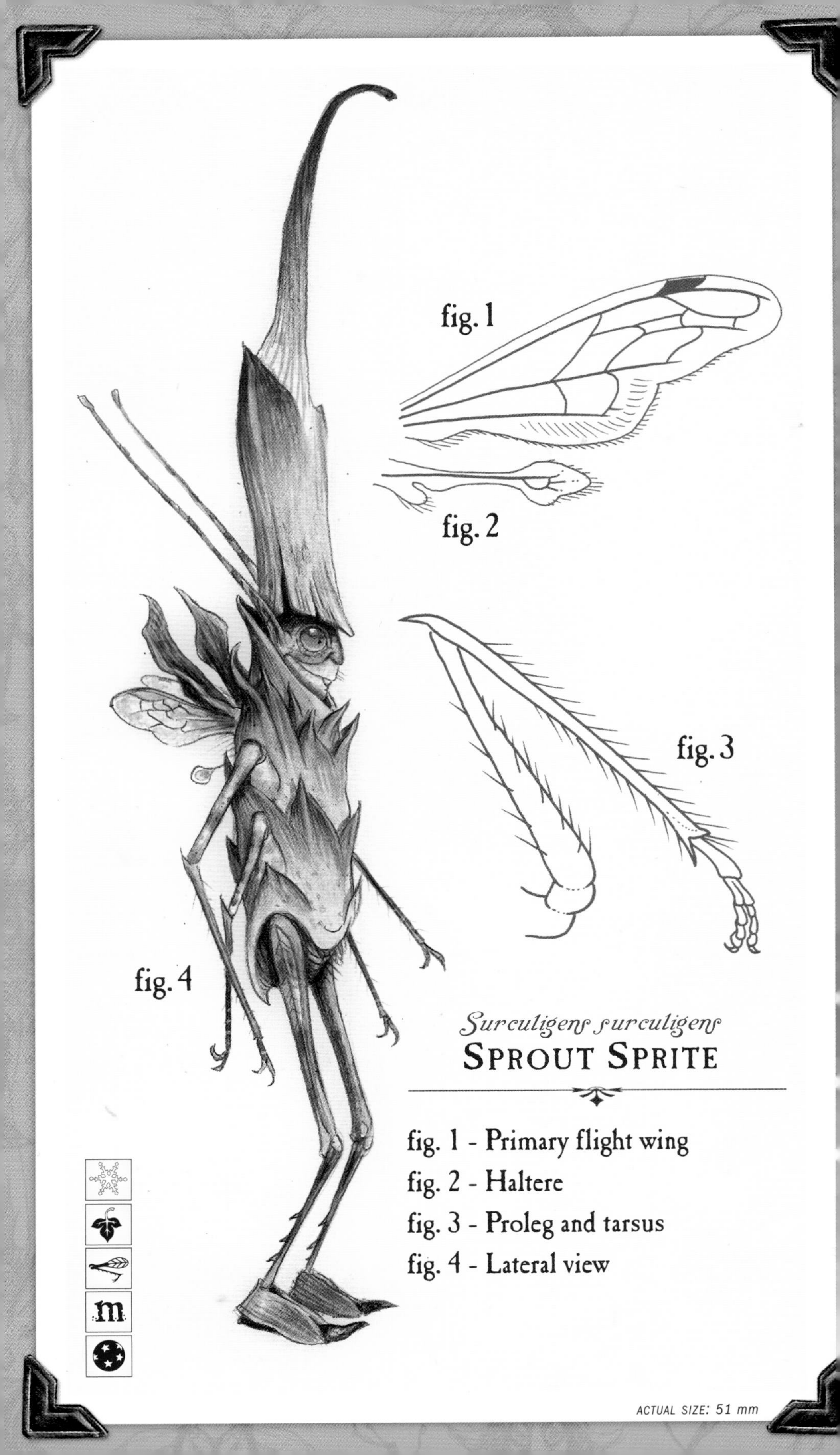
fig. 1
fig. 2
fig. 3
fig. 4
Surculigens surculigens
SPROUT SPRITE
fig. 1 - Primary flight wing
fig. 2 - Haltere
fig. 3 - Proleg and tarsus
fig. 4 - Lateral view
ACTUAL SIZE: 51 mm

ILLNESSES OF SPRITES

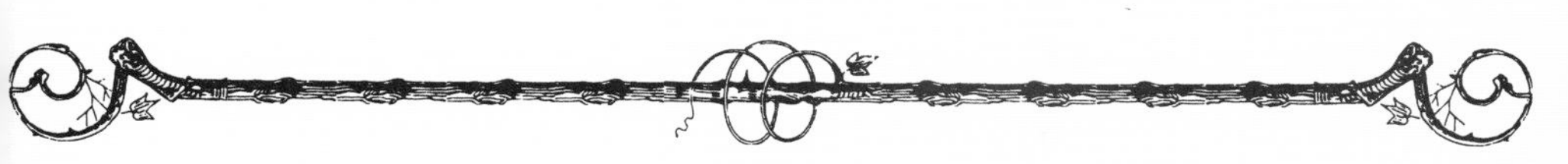

Sprites are violently allergic to chemicals and iron, so be especially careful of metals like steel, which are made with iron. And make sure all cage components are plastic or plastic-covered. Should your sprite become exposed to iron or steel, remove the sprite from where it received the injury and treat the infected area as for a burn. Wash exposed area with cool water or cover with a cool, wet cloth for several minutes. Dress with dry cloth.

Common household chemicals can harm your sprite. Be especially careful to keep your sprite away from bleach, antifreeze, glass cleaner, and paint thinner. If your sprite is exposed to chemicals or has ingested them, you should immediately have it either bathe in or drink warm (but not hot!) milk. If vomiting commences, give small sips of water to rehydrate.

Sprites are generally resistant to most human diseases but do sometimes get ailments that are common to plants. If your sprite looks unwell, you should check for aphids, fungus gnats, thrips, scales, or spider mites and treat with all-natural pesticides.

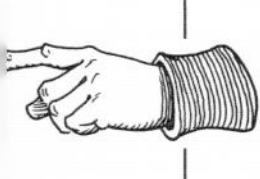

LEFT: Grass and flower sprites seem to have a particular fondness for drinking large amounts of sweet syrups, which always results in an upset stomach.

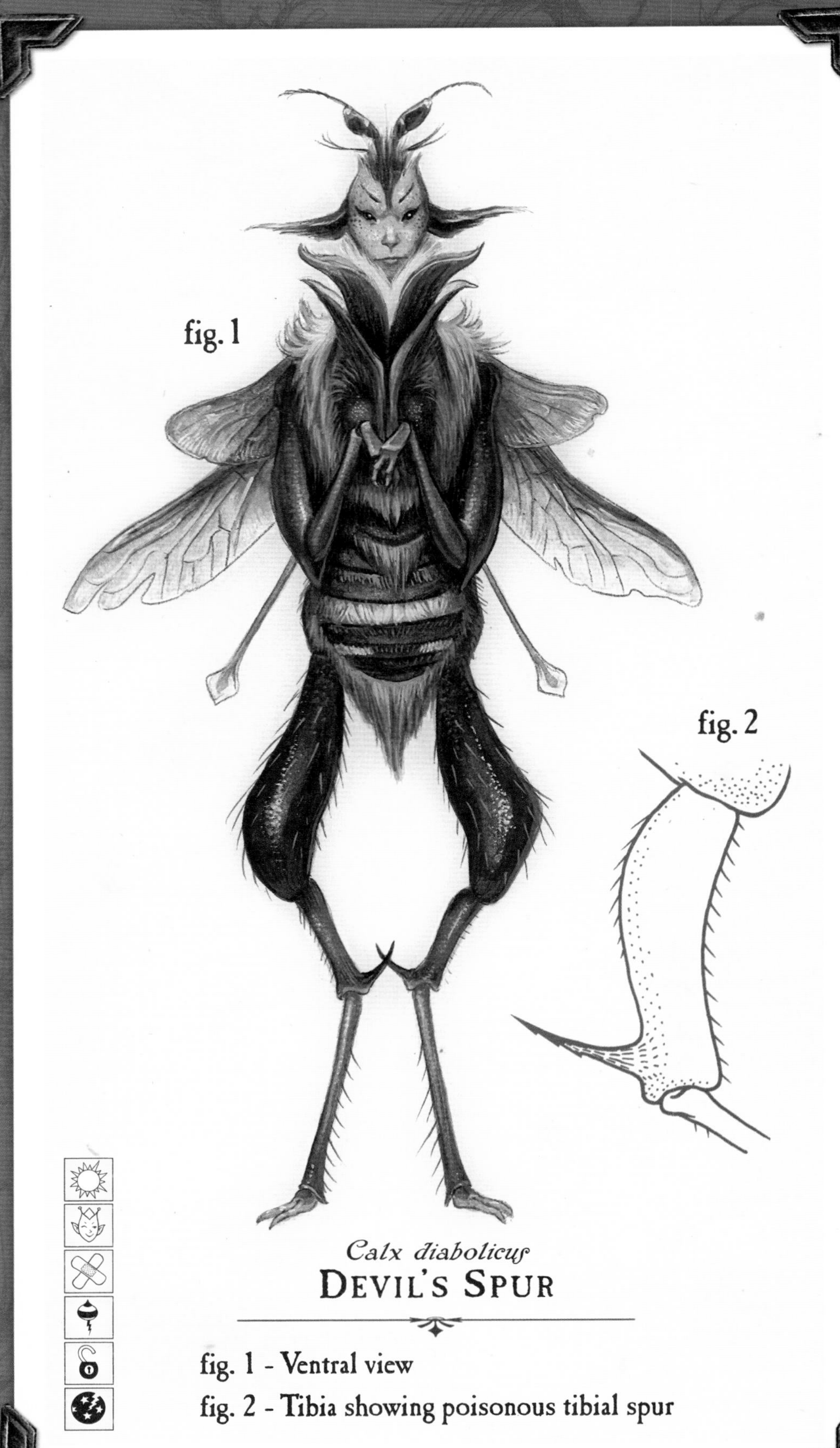

Calx diabolicus

DEVIL'S SPUR

fig. 1 - Ventral view

fig. 2 - Tibia showing poisonous tibial spur

THE MANY MOODS OF YOUR SPRITE

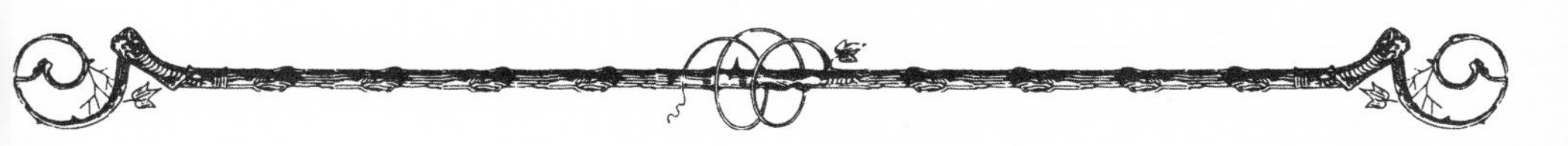

SMILING SPRITE

Scheming

LAUGHING SPRITE

Amused by scheming

FROWNING SPRITE

Scheming

SPRITE MAKING FUNNY FACES

Trying to distract you from evidence of scheming

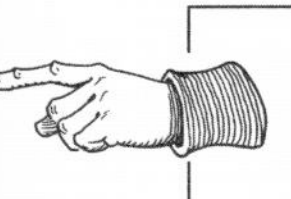

LEFT: Just like bees and hornets, many insect sprites are capable of nasty stings. These sprites are best handled with extreme caution.

KEEPING MULTIPLE SPRITES

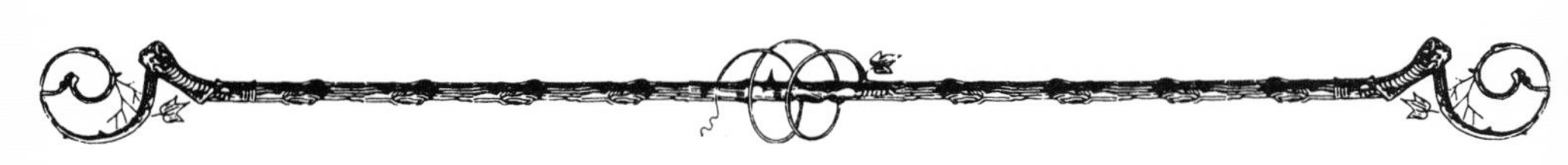

Although one sprite on its own is tricky enough, two or more together can lead to more serious trouble. Even so, sprites are trooping faeries, that is, faeries that enjoy living in large social groups, and will be happier in the company of other sprites.

If keeping more than one sprite, you should provide each individual with separate bedding, clothing, and toys as they cannot be counted upon to share. Also be aware that they may squabble, creating quite a racket. But sometimes squabbling sprites are preferable to sprites that seem to be getting along because when they're working together, you can be sure they're up to something.

IN A GROUP SETTING, YOU CAN EXPECT THAT SPRITES WILL:

- *FROLIC, DANCE, AND SING—SOMETIMES LOUDLY AND OFF-KEY*
- *GOSSIP BEHIND ONE ANOTHER'S BACKS*
- *BRAG*
- *MAKE UP RULES AND BREAK THEM*
- *CALL UPON YOU TO SETTLE THEIR ARGUMENTS*
- *ESCAPE IN A SWARM AND CARRY OFF OBJECTS OF INTEREST OR EVEN INFANTS*

RIGHT: Frogflies and toadflies are the largest of all sprites. They do quite well in captivity and enjoy the company of other sprite species.

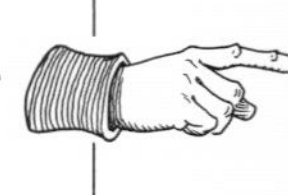

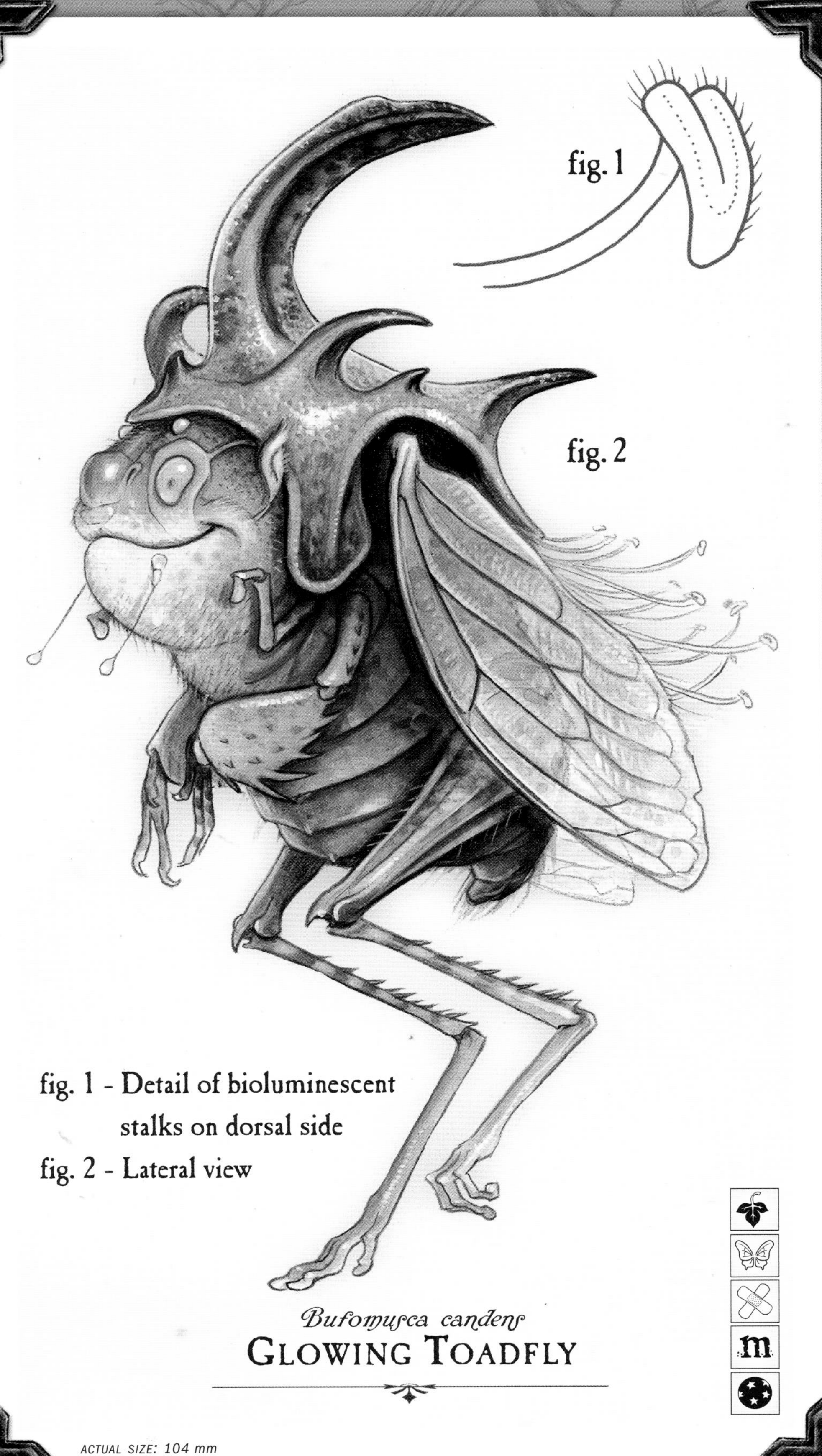

Bufomusca candens

GLOWING TOADFLY

ACTUAL SIZE: 104 mm

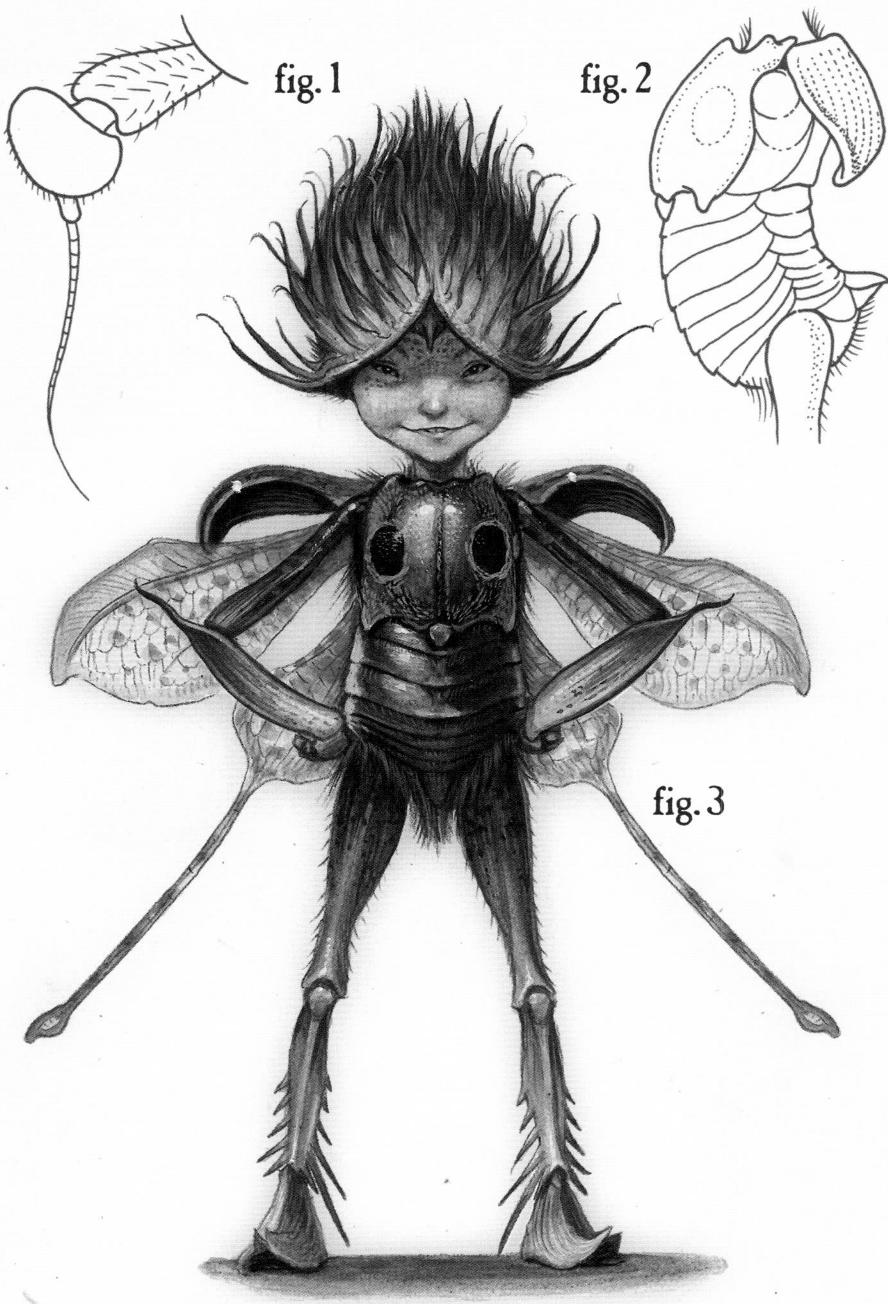

Ala florida

Flower-Winged Sprite

fig. 1 - Detail of antenna

fig. 2 - Lateral view of thorax and abdomen (showing sclerites)

fig. 3 - Ventral view

ACTUAL SIZE: 37 mm

Section Fourteen

REINTRODUCING YOUR SPRITE INTO THE WILD

Sprites live lives far longer than those of humans, so there may come a time when you need to let your sprite go. If so, you should select the area of release carefully. Deep woods, full of oak trees and with a small stream nearby, is an ideal location. Bring some of the sprite's clothing and toys to make reintroduction easier, and be sure to pack up a last lunch for the sprite, as it may need to travel a ways to discover another group of sprites.

One Sprite League member recalls how hard it was to let his sprite go. He was moving to a dorm where there was no room to house his sprite, so he made the difficult decision to release it into a nature preserve. He says he will never forget how its wings shimmered as it flew up toward the clouds, waving to him as it went.

How to Make the Grieving Easier

- *Store your sprite's cage and equipment out of sight so that you don't have to look at them regularly.*
- *Allow yourself to openly express your sadness.*
- *Spend time with other grieving sprite keepers, who will understand what you are going through.*
- *Get involved in new activities and hobbies.*

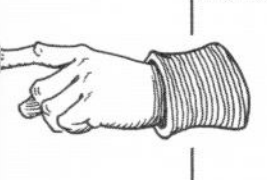

LEFT: Flower sprites usually reside in gardens and meadows. Oftentimes they will remain in one garden patch for many, many years.

SHOWING YOUR SPRITE

You may enjoy joining a sprite club, where members can get together and talk about the special needs and wonderful qualities of the sprite. Occasionally some of these clubs will organize shows, where sprites can be exhibited. Like a cross between a beauty pageant and the Westminster dog show, a sprite show focuses on the judging of sprites' smart outfits, tricks, and overall appearance. Many sprites are said to enjoy these competitions greatly, although some keepers find them abhorrent.

The International Sprite League is the best known of the sprite clubs and has been attracting members at an unprecedented rate over the last few years. The popularity of sprite keeping has inspired the Goblineers Association and the Society of Brownie Fanciers to become better organized and to begin to have competitions of their own.

RIGHT: Beetle sprites are quite agile and, to the delight of many audiences, can perform remarkable acrobatic feats.

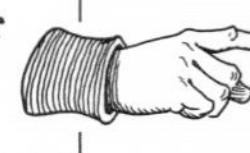

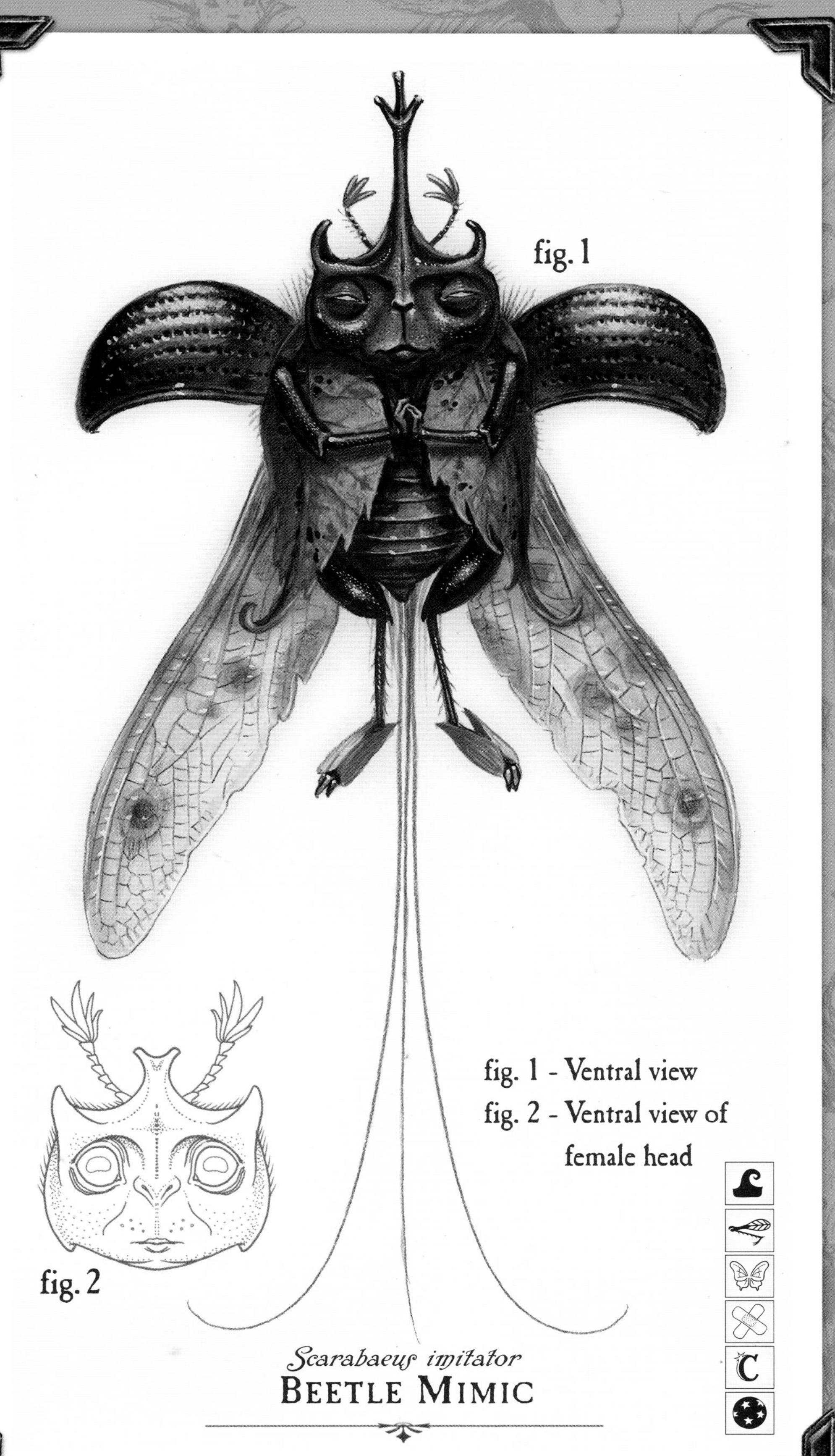
fig. 1
fig. 1 - Ventral view
fig. 2 - Ventral view of
female head
fig. 2
Scarabaeus imitator
BEETLE MIMIC
ACTUAL SIZE: 41 mm

INTERNATIONAL SPRITE LEAGUE

MISSION STATEMENT

OUR PURPOSE is to create positive awareness of sprites as engaging pets and to form a breed standard by which sprites can be shown in competitions all over the world.

OATH OF THE INTERNATIONAL SPRITE LEAGUE

Safety – We will do our best to prevent our sprites from harm and from harming others. We will avoid stings, bites, and scratches. Minimizing the danger of our hobby is our number one objective.

Personable – We promise to be kind, helpful, gentle, and always considerate of the other's feelings. Even if our sprite is never considerate of ours.

Responsibility – A sprite is forever! Since sprites live for an eternity if cared for properly, we are taking on a lifelong responsibility when we choose our pets. We pledge to provide for their basic wellness and for the little things that give our sprites joy.

Integrity – We promise to honor and uphold the principles of the International Sprite League and keep its secrets.

Trustworthy – No, really. We'll keep its secrets.

Excellence – We strive to attain the highest possible standards in all sprite-related activities, including, but not limited to, grooming, food preparation, cage maintenance, and obedience training.